Kluge

Based on a True Story

Tom Baker

Zem Books

Kluge

Based on a True Story

By

Tom Baker

ISBN 978-1-387-49788-1

Zem Books

1.

Kluge woke up that morning, rolled out of bed, went to the sink. He looked in the cracked, yellow mirror, wiped a hand across his eyes, and twisted the little brass knob of the spigot.

A trickle of water fell out into the filthy, cracked Formica. He took a palm full of it, and splashed his face. Outside, the sounds and smells of the city began creeping in through the dirty window panes. He could hear the chug of the El, the honk of myriad horns, someone shouting in the distance; a fight.

Screaming, cursing; what could he do today? Maybe walk to the library. He liked it there, amid the cold and the musty, deep smell of the old books. He liked the silence. No one tried to speak to him when he sat in the stacks, thumbing through picture books and magazines. No one bothered him.

He should walk around, he knew, try to find some work. Odd jobs. That was all that could be expected of him. Cleaning toilets, emptying wastebaskets; mopping floors. Somehow or other, he was always screwing it up, though; always with his foot in the bucket, dropping the can of this or that all over the floor, making a mess. Then, the BOSS would give him his money, get rid of him. "I got enough of what I want from you, you idjit. Now here's a couple of bucks. Get out."

So go he would. And he'd bring the money back home. Bu the bitch usually spent it on booze, he knew, and he went around tightening his belt with a hungry belly, scavaging around in garbage cans, and eating old crusts of stale bread.

"Brother Pete"

Brother Pete worked. He spend ten
hours a day busting heavies at the
warehouse, come home grimey, reeking of
cheap booze, sweat, stale tobacco. He'd
bound up the stairs at midnight, come in, sit
down at the rickety old table, drum his half-
drunk, cracked knuckles against the table.
He's be waiting for Ma to come and ladle

him out some cabbage or boiled potatos, maybe a cheap cut of meat. This was food reserved for her "big, hard-workin' boy." Kluge got whatever was left over.

Then Pete would play solitaire till two, three in the morning. The Vic would be wound up, Ma swaying drunkenly in time to the music. It all made Kluge sick.

He opened the door of his room (which was in reality a walk-in closet) went down the hall--which smelled of insecticide, deep must, rotten food, and a deep indescribable odor cutting through it all. Downstairs, he could hear the WOP neighbor yelling at his wife. Mr. Petrucci, the butcher...

"Maybe one day he'll chop her into cutlets," Kluge laughed to himself. He knew that, soon, the fists would start flying, the woman would start screaming, furniture would start crashing.

He went down the hall, over the creaking floorboards, into the kitchen. He passed Ma's room on the way, and looked

4

in as the door was cracked.

"Ma"

She was bundled into a corner of the sagging mattress. An empty bottle rattled across the floorboards. He looked down. Ghosts? No. A mouse. A mouse moved the booze bottle.

Suddenly, as his eyes adjusted to the light, he saw his brother with one hand hoisted on the window sill. Looking out, smoking, wearing his ratty green workshirt and his sailor cap.

Ma mumbled something. He couldn't quite catch what, but Pete answered in an equally mystifying drawl that Kluge couldn't interpret. He wondered what the hell his brother was doing in his mother's bedroom at this hour, knew better than to ask, and was about to turn from the door when his brother turned, spied him with a suspicious, condescending eye, and said, "Oh, hey dummy. What you up and about so early in the morning for?"

The lump on the bed that was Kluge's mother rolled over, mumbled something incoherent, and pulled the yellowed sheets and threadbare blanket over her thick stringy mop of hair.

Kluge mumbled something, hoping he would miss his brother's wrath. Pete's face was slack with boredom and weariness, but he straightened the end of his rumpled shirt, walked past Kluge at the door, said "I'll make some grits."

6

He made coffee and grits. Kluge went to the counter, took a chipped formica bowl from the cupboard, sat down. He took his twisted spoon, ladled some grits from the pan on the table, poured some bad coffee into an old glass mug.

"You still lookin' for work, bubbelah?" Pete slopped some grits on a piece of black toast, sipped his coffee, grimaced. Kluge didn't know how to respond. He looked at the pale puddle of grits in his bowl, saw a world swimming down there. Wished he could disappear into white static puffiness...

He shrugged.

"Sure. Yeah. I guess so. Maybe I can clean up at the pinball arcade. Maybe. Mr. Lawrence paid me good last time."

"Maybe I can clean up at the pinball arcade. Mr. Lawrence paid me good last time."

Pete chewed his toast reflectively, said "Not a job for a real man, even if he is slow. You gonna be a loafer all your life, or you gonna grow up and learn some goddamned responsibility finally? Ma can't take care of you her whole life."

He could see how bloodshot his brother's eyes were. He was probably coming off his drunk, was tired and mean as hell.

"I'm a get a job soon, Pete. I swears it."

In point of fact, he had no idea if he would or not. But his brother was a mean, ugly sonofabitch when crossed, and Kluge was a weak man.

"Yeah, well, like I said, you wander around town all day--don't try to deny it, everybody knows you and I hear them talk-- and then you come home, and you eat our fuckin' food and live under our fuckin' roof. And what do you do around here to help out? Jack and shit, as far as I can tell.

"Now, I know you're a dummy. Yeah, yeah, go ahead and cry if you want, you feeble-minded fuck. You have to face the truth about yourself sometime--"

Kluge had heard this before, but the description of himself as a "dummy" never failed to sting him, to piss all over whatever happiness he managed to hide, like a forbidden flower, at the core of his being.

"Pete, I try to work. Honest I try. But the bosses don't like me. I try real hard. But they don't like me. They say, 'Stop wasting my time, ya fuckin' idiot!', and they say, 'Don't drop that. No, don't go there! No, pull this lever, not that one!' and then usually they say I broke somethin', and then I'm shitcanned. Aw, I hate it, Pete, but that's the way it is! Aw, I hate it--"

He suddenly WAS crying now, jabbing his big, meaty fists into his eyes as the stinging tears rolled down his cheeks. Pete sat back, belched, rolled a smoke with one gnarled hand, and said, "Well, hell, you're gonna have to find you a job where you ain't a bull in a China shop, is all, I guess. Somewhere doin' somethin' you can't possibly fuck up. Although I have no idea where that could be."

He sniffled, jobbed his eyes with his fists, smiled a dumb grin, and said "I wish I could go to the Navy like you did, Pete. Aw, I wish I could go to the Navy like that, and sail on a boat, and be a Navy man for Uncle

Sam. Aw, Pete, you know I want to go to the Navy."

Pete leaned back in the rickety kitchen chair, dragged on his smoke, actually grinned a little. Then he said, "Yeah, well, the Navy don't take feebs. Sorry. You ain't got what it takes is all. Maybe one of these days, when Ma dies, they'll ship you off to Rockford, or Chatahoochie, or someplace where you can mop floors all day. I guess maybe you'd better see if old Lawrence will give you a few bucks to clean the pinball games..."

Ma came in like a whisper, her energy flooding the room like a wave of static.

"Aw Peter, leave him the hell alone. He tries." She blew into the kitchen, grabbed a coffee mug, and poured a flood of hot mud into her cup, sat down at the table.

"Roll me one too, honey. There's a good boy. Now, damn it, leave your brother alone. Can't you see he's sensitive? He's a sensitive boy!"

She said this as if she had an early-morning mouthful of turd. He said, "Sure am, Mama. Sure. I'm *sen-si-tive*. I'm a good boy. I'm a good boy."

He smiled at his brother. He knew his mother would act as a buffer against his brother's more virulent hatred. For her part, Edwina tolerated her feeble-minded son because occasionally he did work. And he brought home whatever he earned when he could.

"Yes, you are a good boy, honey. Damn it Pete, do you know something? I walked in here, and I could have sworn it was Daryl sittin' there, just as plain as day. Boy, do you realize how much you look like your father?"

It was a few moments later, when Kluge had finished his coffee (which was cold now and tasted terrible) that Ma moved her shaggy-headed self a little closer to Pete, whispered something in his ear; and then, as if to completely defeat the purpose of whispering, looked mischievously sideways at Kluge, and addressing Pete, said "I got a little surprise for you, baby. In the ice box. Been keeping it fresh all day. Oh, it's nice and juicy, red and raw. Cook it up for you later, okay?"

Pete broke into an awkward, embarrassed grin.

"Sure...Ma." he managed to spit.

Even Kluge knew they were talking about food. Something just for Pete, her big strong sailor-man. A steak, maybe. Kluge would get none of it. His stomach began to crawl. He was still hungry.

***

He dimly thought he could hear a baby crying as he walked down four flights of tenement stairs, his eyes adjusting slowly to the gloom. He had heard the same plaintive, ugly baby wail again and again as he trudged down these steps, day after day. Maybe it was a ghost?

No. As dim as he was, even he didn't believe that. But, someone should really do something for that baby; or, he thought, it would surely die. He trudged to the bottom of the stairs, opened the door which squealed and creaked like it had Hell's hinges. To the street.

Outside the street met his ugly, early-mornig gaze with its own crawling life forms. Ratty bums shifted in doorways, pimps and pushers walked, spectral, through fast-disappearing shadows. Amazingly, kids hiked to and from bus stops on their way to public school. He passed a basketball court, where a few lonely teens tossed a ball back and forth.

The court was lined by broken glass, cast-off beer bottles and old tin cans. He once found a girlie magazine here and snuck it home, spent all day looking at pictures of women with huge, surgically-augmented tits and bland, dispassionate faces.

But those faces were frozen, for him, in his memory, screaming from behind their ragged, garish magazine prisons.

For Kluge, a picture was worth a

thousand words. Worlds existed in the tiniest, most minute places. He could look into a handful of dust, and envision a world. A rubbish heap contained the possibility of life just as certain as if it had been the surface of some alien world.

At times, when he was meditating upon the possibility of the existence of such life, his eyes would go blank; his jaw would sag, his face took on a queer, ecstatic expression...and, just once, he had even had a seizure.

More often, though, he let a streamer of saliva hang from his chin. It was this that had gotten him thrown out of department stores and shitcanned from various menial jobs.

"So I was born with a bad cabbage," he often thought to himself. "Jesus loves me, anyway."

He walked down the boulevard until he came to the bus stop. He dug in his pocket, found one thin dime, and smiled. At least he could get off his dogs for a little while.

The bus was crowded with early morning workers, a smattering of English and Spanish competing with the screeing of what sounded like the oldest, scratchiest library recording being broadcast over an old radio.

Past the shops, past the huddled, ugly crowds. He fancied he could see lines of force, lines of electricity crackling off of people's shoulders. These were busy people, he knew: secretaries, cops, file clerks, people with steady jobs and families and lives they went to and fro from. Up in the morning: eggs, toast, coffee. Kiss the wife. Hug the kids. Outside to rev up the family Dodge, and then off to another day in the rat race. Not him. The world didn't want him for any of that.

The bus shuddered and rumblyfarted to its next stop. He pulled the rope above his head to signal where he wanted off at. Just down the walk he could make a few people standing outside of Kaufman's

Pinball Emporium, which was a down-at-the-heels shop with a glass front with PINBALL painted on it in huge circus letters. Outside, he could see One Ear talking to No Legs.

One Ear (thus named because he possessed just one rather striking ear that stood out in rapt attention from the side of his skinny, long, uanppealing face) was known around the neighborhood for lurking outside of schoolyards with pockets full of candy...Of course, no one could ever prove anything. No one ever testified, and the only time he incurred a beef, he walked away from it scott free. Charges dismissed. Same old same old: kid wouldn't testify.

So maybe it was fear. Who knows? No Legs, on the other hand, was a paraplegic lush that scooted around on a little cart with wheels, using his filthy hands to propel him forward. He was, in truth, one of the dirtiest, foulest, filthiest individuals anyone was ever likely to encounter anywhere. His skin, which was nominally white, had long ago soured into a kind of purplish rottenness, and his beard was long and infested and scraggly. His clothes could probably have crawled off of his body by themselves, and to crown it all he wore an absurd sombrero hat that looked as if it had been cast off from the costume department of a bad western epic. His hair was stringy, matted, greasy; every bit as filthy as the rest of him.

"Whew! Boy, you smell so bad, I bet the flies even avoid landing on you."

"No Legs"

No Legs looked up, toothless, guileless, guiltless.

He nods his head stupidly. He produces a paper sack with a bottle in it. Typical day.

"What you got somethin' against me, buddy? Something personal? Don't you know who I am?"

One Ear looked at him askance,

crossing his skinny arms over his chest.

"I suppose next you'll tell me you lost your legs in the war. Right?"

No Legs looked at him, cocked a filthy, crooked grin, and said, "How'd you lose your ear, wise guy? Eatin' pussy?"

One Ear was non-plussed, and said, "Asshole, I was born this way."

"Sure."

The sun painted both of them in a light and shadow dumbshow. Minutes crawled by; time stood still. They were framed by the filthy arcade window.

"A Sailor (with a capital S) came out, a cigarette smoldering in his mouth."

A Sailor (with a capital S) came out, a cigarette smoldering in his mouth His eyes were sinister, slate-grey, and hard. His head as crowned with a sailing cap and a sweat-soaked, filthy bandanna. He wore a small spaghetti-strap teeshirt, and a pair of filthy white Cracker Jack trousers.

"Disrespect me again, I'll kick you right the fuck off that little...whatever that is you're ridin' around."

And because No Legs knew he was not being serious, he said, "Okay shitmobile, I take that back. You ain't had pussy since pussy had you. I bet you lost your ear...I don't know. Maybe you were tryin' to fuck a dog, is all, and maybe it bit your ear off."

"Sure. Better think of a better one, kemosabe. Not likely."

No Legs said, "Well, a man can't very well lose his legs by fuckin' a dog, now can he? But, here, c'mon, let's be friends. Here, you want a swig? C'mon."

He held out a bottle of what looked and smelled to be rancid nectar of piss and turpentine, his filthy hands, wrapped in dirty bandages and crusted gloves with the fingers cut out, shaking a little.

Whether or not One Ear ever took the bottle of poisonous bile and actually drank from it, Kluge never did discover. Inside.

2.

He flipped idly through a comic book. The deep, four-color world of the pictures excited his eyes, and inflamed his mind.

The subject of the comic was obtuse to him. He couldn't read very much of it. But he could tell what was going on by the pictures. As he looked at the little colored panels, he began to see, again, in a real and powerful way, the world inside his head unfold for him, becoming a real, living, and breathing environment, a route of escape from the boredom and sense of nothing.

How many people, for instance, could visit a world wherein the secretaries of a typical newspaper office were cowering outside the boss' door, too scared to enter?

"We can't possibly go in there," one of them squeaks. "I mean, for chrissakes, look at the man! His head exploded into some sort of...of...cosmic void? Infinite gateway? Oh, heavens to Betsy, I just don't know how to label it, Donna!"

Donna (quite a looker with her long

legs, blonde bombshell hairdo, and torpedo tits) says, "He's already ingested the water cooler, all the ashtrays, the tea kettle, a small Frigidaire, and the copy boy! What could possibly be next?"

Dan (the Man) , the unofficial office lothario says, "If this door doesn't hold, we're all toast! Jeepers, whatever can we do against a...a...SPACE BEETLE?"

That was the name of the comic. SPACE BEETLE. Kluge liked it better than any of the others he picked up second-hand, in alleyways, on the bus. The main character was a guy whose head exploded into some sort of doorway in space (to the reader, maybe what is typically referred to as a "black hole" or even a "wormhole").

This guy was a reporter or something. He was a bigshot, Kluge knew, and whenever he sensed the presence of an evildoer, his SPACE BEETLE head exploded into that flaming flower, and the evildoer was sucked into another world.

(The reader is advised to imagine a

man whose intense concentration on all matters psychic leads to his eventual possession by a force determined to use his brain as a gateway for otherworldy retribution. This force, in later installments of the comic, is revealed to be the Initial Spark of consciousness that lead to the creation of the known universe. But Kluge didn't know any of this.)

There were some comic scenes at first, when Mr. Wormhole was riding in the back of a cab, trying to keep his head from exploding into an interdimensional vacuum cleaner--

"...From which no light could ever escape." Kluge mouthed the words, his dry, cracked lips moving silently. He could read that. It was slow, plodding, but it surprised even him. Around him, the silence of the library was suddenly deafening; his stomach rumbled and complained about his hunger. He folded the comic and stuffed it (much as he stuffed other items) under the waistband of his shirt. He decided to head home, pushing out the door and adjusting back to the outside world again.

"I read those words," he said to himself. "Big words. I'm gettin' to be a big boy."

Sen-is-tive, as Ma would say.

Outside, standing at the corner, he saw the same skinny black girl standing, smoking a cigarette. She hadn't noticed him come out of the library.

He had had a dream the night before. Been in a small town. Whole place looked deserted.

Inside, there was a girl lying on a bed, covered in bandaids. Maybe she looked familiar to him, maybe she didn't. Hadn't he seen her somewhere before? He wasn't sure. All he knew was that, in his dreams, he was an entirely different person.

(He was a lot better looking, for one thing, His whole face, he knew, bore the aspect of a burrowing aardvark. Someone kinder to themselves might have suggested a tapir, but he didn't think he could very

26

well go around as a "tapir man," so he imagined himself a mole. He imagined himself a lot of things, but here, in the world of dreams, he was forever on the cusp, at least, of obtaining the thing he wanted.

The house seemed curiously empty. Very little furnishings.

"Are we hiding out here?" he might have asked her. He could never remember much dialogue from his dreams. The girl might have rolled around in bed, her body smelling sweaty and stale under the rumplead sheets. But, for all that, still desirable he thought. He was not particular.

She was partially unclothed. Curiously, he observed this in a detached way; this would have, otherwise, exited him, were he to witness it anywhere besides here.

Outside, the town was a barren road flanked by eighteen hundreds buildings, rusted, piece-of-shit cars, and houses falling over onto their sagging porches. Houses that seemed badly in need of paint, with vacant, sobre, eye-like windows looking out in black derision at the casual observer sauntering by; seeming to say, "I dare you to look behind my walls, to see into the guts of my hideous life," as the little insects crawl lazily back and forth across the floorboards.

But this house had white walls, plastered down with heavy spackel and fresh paint.

He walked in and out of the empty rooms. Behind the door, she sprawled across the mattress, her hair disheveled and dirty, and hanging in short strings from her too-pretty face. The eyes were bright blue, the cheeks prominent, lips full. Breasts heavy; rumpus gone to fat. The skin was pale, even pasty.

"I understand I've come here to marry you." He said it flatly, plainly, lying next to her.

"I understand I've come here to marry you."

He said it flatly, plainly, lying next to her.

Some friends had dropped him off, apparently. This was just some pissant burg, seventy miles outside the city. He didn't want to be late to his own wedding

She never replied with any words he could remember. He wasn't sure whether or not they made love, but in time, he found that he had gotten up out of the bed, wandered outside.

It was mostly hillbillies that lived here, he thought to himself. Good, stolid, country folk. Not like the degenerate pigs in the city, where junk and gangs ruled the streets. He breathed in lungs full of fresh air, breathing deep, exhailing as if the very act of taking in God's Fresh Clean Small Town All-American Country Air was enough to reinvent him, heal what was wrong with him. But, all the same, he felt like the people he couldn't see, the people hiding behind locked doors and silent, black windows, were all watching him intently, their eyes crawling across his form as he walked down little streets, through neighborhoods silent and bleak, with drooping trees in littered front yards, toys and games and dolls left, like battered orphans, on overgrown front lawns.

The occasional tire swing hung down like a disused noose. He fancied he could see a little moppet, invisible, perhaps the ghost from someone else's past, sitting like a lonely wraith in the rubber donut mouth.

Lonely emptiness choked this deserted mecca of small town USA values and ideals. So silent, he fancied he could could hear water dripping down the alley.

Suddenly, as he rounded a corner, the sun appearead to be blotted out by the image of three men. Heavy, burley shitkickers, small town types with monstrous builds and tremendows fat bellies, hidden by faded blue overalls. Each could have been a twin or clone of the other, with their red and white checked flannel shirts, straw hats, heavy, pudding-dull faces. Salt of the Earth, they must have been, and walking behind them was a weirdly mystical experience, with the slanting beams of sunlight shining through their shoulders.

"But why do they walk so close together, side by side?" he asked himself.

One of them took off his hat, wiped a bandanna across his forehead as if the sweat was getting to him. But it was not warm.

The scenee cut-jumped to a pleasant row of houses at the edge of main street. Suddenly she (the bedridden girl he had been dropped off here to marry) was standing beside him, pointing to a low domicile.

"Good," he said to her. "I don't think I could have found my way back."

As if she had not been listening to him, she said, "Over there, I live over there now. Silly."

Next, they were in the kitchen, which was more or less simply a bar and a swinging door. Someone in brown overalls was standing at the stove, cooking chicken. He totally ignored Kluge.

"Maybe he can't see me," Kluge said to himself. At any rate, even though he wasn't hungry, he found himself picking up a plate. The man turned, ladled a piece of chicken on to Kluge's plate, turned back to the stove.

"I just got off my job at Tire Shack," he said, as if talking to no one in particular. Kluge looked around, suddenly realizing how filthy the kitchen was. Regardless, he spied a better, larger piece of chicken, only barely touched, on a dirty plate. "Well, if I'm going to be part fo the family now..." he said to himself, picking up the piece and trading it for the inferior piece he had been given by the man.

"This is my fiance," she said. She hadn't moved a muscle since he had entered the room. The man in the brown overalls seemed understanding, if somewhat menacing. Or, maybe he was just trying to contain the lurking anger and violence Kluge sensed was buried, like a submersible, beneath his pale skin.

They all tried to squeeze onto the sordid mattress with THEIR girl. None of

them were nude, but it was a dirty,
uncomfortable fit.

3.

(Note: The personal memoirs of Kluge
Stinton have been edited for easier
readability. Otherwise, they are unaltered.)

He picked up a pen, picked up a piece
of paper. Scrawled, in ignorant, grade-
school letters a mountain high:

The Policeman blew his whistle, and
the band played on...

Now, what in the hell did that mean?
He had no idea. His scruffy noggin was
always popping out obscurities and strange,
jingle-jangle rhymes, nonsense mutters. It
was because, he figured, he had no one else
to talk to.

The door goes bang. It goes bang,
bang. It goes bang, bang, bang.

Like a gun, he figured.

His skills at writing were getting
better.

He picked up the pen again, brushed

a fly that was circling, with dumbshow horror, to the greasy end of his nose, and he started writing again. Faster this time. What else did he have to do?

"When I walked in on them from the street, I could hear the moaning and grunting. Momma said sinners and whores moan and grunt like that, and all sinners and whores go to hell. I don't know. Maybe I will go to hell.

"I think Papa is in Hell. Maybe he is smoking that cigar with old Nick Scratch. Yeah, I remember that cigar in the tips of his fingers. His fat fingers, and he bending over me in the crib, and getting closer and closer and I'm crying. And it smokes from the tips of his fingers, and I think it is a big bug sticker, and anyway I'm still crying, so why doesn't he stop? But he brings that smoking tip down into my face, and the smoke gets in my lungs and right away I feel the bright hot flash of pain as it burns like a cherry red root deep into my face and Oh! God! i'll never forget that pain. Or being crouched in the dark, and hearing him breathe and walk the floor. Clack and pound went the boots and shoes against the wood, and I am crouched in the darkness breathing, and he's out there in the dark, and he's gonna spank me for getting my pants wet again. For wetting the bed. And so I am crouched in the dark and it is hot and flies are dying around my crotch, and I can smell the piss in my trousers, but I can smell fear and hatred, too..."

He put his pen down. The big iron door slammed shut outside. Voices murmured and shouted, echoing through the corridors, but it was all of one in his mind. Peaceful calm stole down around him like the grey shadows clinging to the cement walls, to the steel bunks; creeping into everything here, a sentinel watching over the dark hidden in its bosom. Everything here was one shade of ashen grey, fading to black.

Rumbling voices. A few shafts of dripping sundown streaked their fugitive way through the barred windows. His belly crawled with acid but a new wave of cold settled over him to soothe him. His cramped fingers were delivering him from the moment. In peace, his mind could wander.

"I don't know why I done what I done..."

He stopped. How much of this did he want to let them know? Weren't these his secrets? But, somehow, he knew he must get it down before his time ran out. Before it was too late to make anyone understand.

"I don't think I could have done it. I think it must have been someone else inside me, some...demon. Maybe the whole place was filled with devils and demons."

On his desk was a large book he had taken from the prison library. His reading had gotten better, but there was very little in the Encyclopedia of Witchcraft and Demonology he could make out and really comprehend. He had liked the pictures though and picked up on the stark horror of

Medieval woodcuts depicting the tortures and terrors of supposed witches and heretics. In one of them, a man was bent over a tree stump, his legs being pressed by hot pincers.

Kluge fancied they could do it to him. Might do it to him, given half the chance. He closed his eyes, his pencil stub scraping along the surface of the paper.

"...here I am home. Here I am back where I belong. Here I am walking into the house. And I can hear the grunting and moaning, and Ma is talking to Bub. And I don't know what's going on at first. And they have to hear me walking in, because they always said I stomped like an elephant, and the floors are wood. And so they can hear me come in. And they don't stop. Maybe they can't stop. But I walk down the hall to tell them about my day, and I don't know what's going on. What do I know about what's going on? So the door is cracked, and I can hear the moaning and grunting and like pigs, and I think maybe someone is sick in there, but it doesn't hit me until I actually adjust my eyes in the light from the window, and it's pretty bright in there, pretty white, but I was coming in from a real dark place..."

He stopped for a moment. Down the corridor, he could hear moaning. Some guy getting it, his cellie giving it to him nice and slow. Kluge knew it would be a short time before he had a new cellie. He couldn't be in this "pent-house suite" by himself, forever.

He tried to imagine what the two hairy oafs, grunting and groaning in the sweaty, humid darkness, would look like. He couldn't picture it; it was, to be perfectly honest, an unseemly pose.

"...but I must have blacked out or something. The devil reared up in me to see it, swam up from the darkness. But, the Devil was all around that place. Pete was getting up from the bed, pulling up his pants, and Ma was laying there spread like some cheap roadhouse whore. She'd been getting a good, slow, hard pimp screw from Pete. And something inside of me couldn't make my mind understand that what I was seeing was really true. But it was..."

The police report had described the altercation in clipped, barely-literate prose, the unromantic, gradeschool-level stuff proffered by minds whose preoccupation was NOT the conjuring of striking literary images: "Suspect fell and/or was pushed back through the doorway by decedent. Altercation ensued. Heard by neighbors. Suspect claims next few minutes experienced as a quote blackout unquote. Statement to the effect that he remembers nothing else that ensued until coming around in custody sometime later."

And on and on. But he had been telling the truth.

Mostly.

The blackout?

It was a cloud of dark, withering rage.

"Pete come at me through the door, and he is yelling, but I no longer am listening to what he is saying. He is back of my head, and he is yelling loud, and I turn around, and I can see his mouth moving. See his teeth moving like rotten, black little stumps in his head, and he just looks like a monster to me. Just a monster. And his face and jaw are so wide and tight, and like a sailor man from a movie.

"So I don't know where the next few minutes come from, because everything is like a jump-cut from an old movie, like from an old movie back twenty years ago, when everyone went around with white faces and dark eyes, and mouths moved but all you hear is some piano music in the back ground, and everything is moving at herky-jerky, topsy-turvy speed, and a car comes around and a bunch of cops in tall hats like rounded tits on their heads fall down and scatter like bugs..."

He smiled in spite of himself. His cracked grin would have shocked anyone who happened upon him in the dark. But for now he was alone.

But Peter was chasing him through the room, he knew, and suddenly he was sliding on the kitchen floor...

"...And I go sliding on the floor and I put my arms out, and I crash into the table. Boom! And the table tips over. And Pete is on top of me, but I don't see as why he should be on top of me, and hitting me, and I am bleeding in the mouth, and I ain't done no wrong, and Pete and Ma, they were the ones doing...doing..."

He must have flailed on the filthy, cracked, linoleum. His mouth was a bleeding mess, his head was thumping against the tiles like a melon. The pain shot up behind his eyelids, making his skull rock. He put out his hand.

"And the Devil himself must have handed it to me because before I knew it, I had that old hatchet..."

"And the Devil himself must have handed it to me, because before I knew it, I had that old hatchet what was thrown under the kitchen sink and we use to cut wood with for the stove back ten years ago...How did it get out there on the floor, within reach? Did the Devil put it there? It's a real mystery."

And he brought that hatchet up, and suddenly, like a scene from a nightmare, from a dream which he couldn't help reliving, again and again, his eyes closed as he cowered in bed, the hatchet was stuck deep in the white, sweaty forehead, and splatering rivulets of blood were seeping out across the white flesh, and Pete reeled backward.

His arms worked stupidly in the air, his grasping, cracked fingernails trying to find purchase against the curved wooden handle. He was too shocked to even yell; it was all dumb-show silence. Blood splashed down upon the cracked, yellowd linoleum.

Kluge got up, his eyes wide. Perhaps exultant. His heart hammered in his chest, blood and snot dripping down his face. His hair was a sodden mass of grease and sweat, and his shirt was stained with blood. If he would have looked in a mirror at this moment, he would have been shocked at the weird, beaten, exultant thing huffing and puffing as it stood there. His hands and fingers tingled with electric energy as he saw Pete settle down into the dying repose in which crime scene photographers and detectives would mark him later in a chalk outline graffito. And that was the end of Brother Pete.

"I still had the hatchet in my hand. But how did I get the hatchet in my hand when it was in Pete's head? I don't know, it was like we skipped a scene. But I was walking through pools of blood, and leaving footprints. Ma's bedroom was awful quiet, but I sensed I was going in there. I could smell smoke. She was smoking heavy, perhaps listening for what was going on, but she had no idea.

"But all I had to do was follow the trail of smoke..."

So he went into the bedroom. Lying like a cheap two-dollar whore across the bed, his mother sat with a long, skinny filtered cigarette in her teeth. She looked at the blood streaked across his shirt, his pants, his bloody footprint trail; his bloodied, seeping face. In his hand, he still held the hatchet.

She didn't respond in the way he imagined she would. She calculated risks behind stupid, greedy, terrified eyes, eyes he suddenly realized were too squinting and pig-like.

"I-I..." she began. She seemed to trail off into the echoing silence of the room. It was bright outside, the sunshine seeping in to blot out the harsh contours of the dun-white walls, the chipped plaster, the cheap, crooked prints. Her cut-outs from film and fashion magazines, the dead and dying bugs on the windows and walls.

He looked at her, and he couldn't reason, suddenly, exactly what she was. His head swam in a moment of unreality, as she cleared her throat, and started again, "There's no need to, no need to do anything you're gonna regret later, okay? We can take care of this, all of this. No one ever needs to find out. Oh, you want to hurt me, is that it? Well, I don't blame you. I let him put his hands all over you, whip you, beat you and burn you....That scar on your face? Yeah, you remember. That big old cigar was like a big red eye of fire, coming down to you from above. Wasn't it that way, honey?"

He stalked around the room. His head was swimming in a halo of blood. Between the filmy sash of her nightgown, he could see her milk-white legs splayed. And then, with smoke billowing out of it, like a crimson cloud of blood, he could see her dirty, shit-colored thing.

"C'mon, c'mere, honey. You feel bad, right now. Momma can make you feel good again, Momma can kiss the troubles away. Come on. C'mere. Give mama a great big kiss."

She writhed on the bed like a snake, the smoke billowing out from her body. He felt his mind crack in rage, the blood streaming down his pale face and pooling in the crook of his neck, splattering and staining the front of his white shirt. And, to blot out this smoking nightmare, this foul, sluttish thing from the pit, he brought the hatchet down with killing intensity, and at that moment he not only split her skull in half, he opened up a crack in the face of the world.

Again, and the blood splattered the wall, soaked the sheets, and still she writhed in her brimstone fury.

The policemen would gag; one of them lost his lunch. She was photographed, repeatedly, splayed across the bed, a butchered rag, a real mess for the morgue wagon and cleanup guys.

He would be cuffed, lead out in a daze. Thrust into a cell, his head still bleeding, a doctor would be finally called in. His wounds were cleaned with burning antiseptic, smelled like bug spray. A loose linen bandage would be wrapped around his head. He would recline, the intense, searing agony he was experiencing in some place, some hole far beyond him. Kluge, they would know later as "The Man Who

Laughed."

The "Boy With the Idiot Grin."

"The Cackling Killer..."

Other noms de plumes were less stellar or dramatic, he supposed. The other cons would call him out through gritted, dirty mouths, and make kissy-poo at him. Spit and throw cups of urine.

Later, they put him in a place so no one could get to him. And he was still smiling.

***

But, before all of that, he had tried to make it with the colored whore that stood on the corner of Merman Ave. Cars honkety honking in the distance, and he coming out of the library spied her, with a comic book rolled around in his pocket.

A little drool dribbled off of his chin.

"This comic book is important," he had tried to explain to her. He whipped it out of his pocket. She was standing there in her little checked skirt, her red purse dangling from one arm, and he started to flip the pages back and forth.

"You see, there's a secret buried somewhere in these pages. And I'm going to find it."

He held out his hand, suddenly. He wanted to feel her hand, feel if she was as real and alive as what she appeared to be.

"Sure. Sugar, what you mean you got some kind of secret in there? Like a code or something?"

He smiled. She could tell by his leer and his gaze he was feeble. Crazy or something.

"Damn, you talk like you're cokey. You ever, you know..."

She put her fingertips to her nostrils, and sniffed as if she had a cold. He found himself fascinated by the long, fake fingernails, chipped and a garish shade of pink, which adorned her slim, lovely fingers.

Also, she wore an assortment of cheap rings.

***

thing. A walking patchwork of fractured tissue and scarred flesh.

The comic book story has been addressed here before. The Boss of the *Daily Grinder* is suddenly, inexplicably, turned into a yawning ripple in the fabric of time and space, his head blossoming in four-color verisimilitude to a warping cosmic wormhole, a place where all matter is sucked straight in, in which all energy is refined to a white-hot point. Lana Suzanna, his plucky secretary, swore, "I won't leave

51

you, boss, not for love nor money! Ya hear me?" and then she'd pop a Chesterfield or Viceroy in the side of her too-dark bee-stung 1938 lips, and curl up one flabby, shapeless strong arm like Rosie the Riveter. After all, she was the spunky spitfire that always got her story, the office equivalent of Madcap Mabel Normand. Maybe even Louise Fazenda.

But Bossman had to wear a peculiar lead hood to keep the juju flames from crisping anyone within eyeshot. Juan Domingo, his driver and Man Friday, had taken to wearing lead goggles and a special leather uniform he thought might protect him.

"Hey, Juan , pull up there. I spot someone that needs the sort of justice that only the Space Beetle can dispense!"

And he would jump from the car on these excursions, march boldly over to some two-bit petty thug harassing some terrified old woman, and the thug would invariably turn around with a sneer. Get smart.

"Hey, Pops, what you think this is? Trick or treat time! Har har!"

This punk smelled of cheap hooch, smelly armpits, and unwashed ass. A cigarette dangled from one end of his thick, ugly liver lips. Boss Space Beetle took the cigarette from his mouth and crushed it between insensible fingers. Behind them, the old woman the thug had tried to molest was walking away as fast as her ancient legs and a cane would carry her.

"Hey mother!" the rotten punk spat from between rotten teeth. "You shouldn't have done that man! Now you're going to pay!"

The punk pulled his requisite switchblade. The Space Beetle slowly took off his hood. In the four-color universe of little stacked panels one atop another, his unholy head bloomed like an orange and yellow flower.

Daddy handed him the axe. On the bed, She was laid out in resplendent decay.

Her mouth was a grimacing Death's Head, a piratical image ripped from a black flag. The image invaded his mind suddenly. Above him, the lightbulb flickered, but he supposed it could have just been the bug,

(the Beetle)

caught in the light fixture. He thought of writing it all down again, but he didn't really know why he should bother. Who would ever read it? He would rather be in the world of the Space Beetle.

Daddy had stuffed the whore under the bed. He remembered her raspberry smile, the trickles of blood sliding easily down the sides of her face as she reclined on the bed, her arms thrust back behind her head. He had taken the body, the smoke still trailing off of it in thick, nauseous plumes.

***

"Smells like farts, Daddy."

Daddy turned, his grin big and black and all-encompassing. You could eat up a world with that grin. You could send planets

54

swirling off into space with the power of that grin. More Death's Head.

"It's brimstone junior. We're in hell. Heads explode outward, bloom like flowers in the sun, burn up nice and crisp. Things like that, they draw something into their orbit, and they don't let it go..."

He shifted on his bunk. Outside, down the hall, he could hear someone murmuring. Someone groaning. Was he praying? Kluge didn't know. They would come for him soon. He knew he had a big appointment today.

***

They had him up against the wall. The punk with the greasy blonde hair was giving him a series of lefts and rights. Ones and twos in his roly poly gut. Hurt like mad, an explosive pain that sent his eyes rolling up into his head, his mouth drooling open, and he yelled. A gloved hand, smelling like dirty crotch and motor oil, was thrust across his mouth.

"Shut your fucking pie hole, retard!

Look, you didn't see nothing, okay? You got that? Nothing. Right? Now just say that, and we can stop, and we can all go home and take a nap."

And Kluge, who had no idea what it was he didn't see, just nodded his shaggy head, tears streaming from his eyes.

"Oh shit, look..."

One of the thugs pointed at the crotch of Kluge's pants, where a huge piss stain was spreading like a blooming flower of stench. A few giggles shot forth, but the blond boy who had been beating him stepped back. A disgusted look on his face.

"Okay retard," he said, giving Kluge a little slap across the cheek with one gloved hand. "I think you get the idea. Now, for God's sake, go change your pants."

They disappeared like characters in a dream, melting into the dark fabric of the alleyway. Kluge groped his tired, dirty way down the wall. In the filthy crease of the back window of the pinball arcade,

Goldblatt's face shined out like half a yellow moon, his mouth hanging slightly open. When he saw Kluge coming, it fell open a little more, the face growing shocked, as if Kluge were a particularly vicious dog approaching from behind the glass. The yellow half-moon face disappeared behind the glass, sinking into the darkness in back.

It was while sitting on his bunk that Kluge had opened the paper to that same face. Arrest. Something about betting, illegal betting on pinball machines. There was a picture of Goldblatt being lead away, his goatish old face showing weary if suppressed outrage. Kluge folded the paper, and put it beside his bunk.

The lights flickered. He knew, in a few minutes, the preacher would come in. Sit beside him. Offer him an opportunity to pray.

Today was a big day for him. Why?

He felt he knew. It was like something int he center of his forehead, which he kept trying to see but was just out of reach of his cross-eyed vision. He picked up his comic.

A blooming head. A universe inside a skull. A man walking around with a bag, a mask over his face, to hide the killing intensity of that light; to stop that black hole vacuum suck that pulled everything into it, and never let it go.

Was he just born bad? Did men fly about the cosmos, from one life to another, from one place to another, just to prove something? His hands beat out a tattoo rhythm against his bunk. The lights flickered. Shadows fell silent across the wall.

He closed his eyes. Ahead of him, two mountainous men walked down the long, lime-green tiled hall, and his mind flashed back to the dream.

Two walking mountains with hats. Ahead of them, the sun, or The Space Beetle's glowing, golden face, shining, making shadows dance at those backs. He was walking, escorted between these two huge mooks. He was going.

"Blessed are the poor in spirit, for they shall be spat upon..."

A voice hissed at his right elbow. Like a serpent. The Chaplain. "Blessed are the meek and lowly, for they shall inherit NOTHING..."

He walked on baby legs, about to be reborn. Inside the mouth of a muttering room, wherein voices from executions past still echoed in some far-off, distant dimension, the black and skeletal bones of the electric chair waited with singed straps and bile on its seat.

Behind a two-way mirror, press.

But he fancied he could see the witnesses.

No one was to have a camera. Forbidden. But, like the Snyder-Grey case of a few years before, someone did have one concealed.

(Snyder and Grey were lovers, yadda yadda. Snyder, Ruth, put Grey, Judd, up to killing her husband, Snyder, Albert, and making it look like a burglary. Gray did so, but the cops not being convinced it was anything other than a cold-blooded homicide of a marital partner, to obtain a double-indemnity life insurance payout. They swooped in, and the murderous paramour coughed up a steady stream of confessions. Coming to Christ, he confessed his sins before God, the detectives and the District Attorney, going gladly into the mouth of the bitter, hungry clown called Fate. Mrs. Grey, the plain, portly widow, was less forthcoming, but the resultant trial saw them both point their fingers at the other. In the end, Fate saw them both into the waiting yaw of the cold, grimacing death chamber, a place where the witnesses were forbidden to capture the resultant executions on film, as that would just be overstepping the boundries into what could be considered "bad taste."

Notwithstanding this attempt to modulate the morbid sensibilities of a sensation-starved public, an enterprising reporter managed, through dint of a cunning, curiously ingenious nature, to rig a sort of "shoe camera" device to his leg, with the operating cord running up his pant leg and into his panting palm. Mrs. Grey was brought in, a hefty little bundle of black nerves, into the execution chamber. A bizarre, grim ceremonial mask was thrust over her face, looking, to the casual observer, like some sort of barabaric ritual enacted around a bonfire by savages, perhaps flesheaters from some far-off, lost tropical isle.

Perhaps she was a goddess. In her last moments, one wonders what she possibly could have felt, if she was fucked by the tickling beard of the electrical serpent if anyone in the witness box was aroused or excited by her slightly thrust-open collars, the smiling part of her heavy, milk-white thighs. The implied pornography of the final, killing image.)

Kluge was strapped in, heavily; he was pregnant with confusion. They had shaved his curly, thick locks; someone had put brine on his temples and attached the electrodes. The cap was a metal helmet, a tight fit.

He wondered if he would mess his pants. He wondered if his head would catch fire. Yeah. that was the ticket; explode into a bright glowering inferno, a cosmic whirlpool dragging in everything in its wake, eating the blessed world.

Just like the Space Beetle.

Behind the glass, a thousand watermelon grins erupted as the skull fire licked his temples. He faded out, still seeing the two great mountainous undertakers preceding him, carrying his casket forth.

Warden Wharton looked through as much dross as he detected spread across the surface of his already flummoxed desk. Bill Bailey had come in, unloaded a thick basket full of the stuff after they had tossed the cell. The possessions of the dead--

"All in his mind. Look here, this confession. All in his mind. I tell you, Bill, the boy was innocent."

Bill wandered around the office, a gin and tonic in one hand, a cigar in the other, He sat down heavily in a high-backed leather chair from 1899.

"Innocent, shit. We had his fingerprints all over the apartment where he killed that colored whore. He wanted her, wanted her in a way he could never have her. So he choked the life out of the bitch, and stuffed her under the mattress. She could stay there, draw flies or mice, it's all the same to me with shines. But, murder is murder Cece. Murder is murder."

"Ayup," Cece Wharton swallowed his drink, and chased it down with bicarbonate of soda and a drop of chocolate. Hard on the stomach,

"What about the mother and brother rap? Suppose?"

Frank looked confused, said "I'm confused, Cece. We talking about the same man now, right? Killed the whore? The colored whore? What's this about a mother and brother?"

Cece snubbed out his cigarette, looked somewhat perturbed. Another drink or two, and he would be mollified. Rolled up in one freckled, cheese-colored fist was a copy of the comic book Space Beetle, a popular title. He said, "My kid reads this. Some damn thing about outer space scientists. Exploding heads in outer space. I don't know."

Frank said, "I could have sworn what he told us there was true. Didn't we have a case of mother-son incest? Murder-suicide, maybe? There's something playing around the edge of my memory, Cece, something ugly and turdly." Turdly was a neologism Frank frequently employed to show an extra filip of consternation or disgust for something, some round peg that didn't fit into his preconceived square hole.

Warden Wharton, Cece to his friends, slammed down his shot glass and said, "See, there, you're doing it again!"

To which Frank replied innocently, "Doing what, pray to tell?"

Cece retorted, "Confusing the past with the future, fantasy with reality, one thing for another thing. Apples and oranges are both fruit, you know..."

He picked the comic book up and flipped it open. A man with an exploding galaxy for a head greeted him from a four-color world contained in neat, vertical panels, word balloons floating up and down the bleeding, inky pages. Well-thumbed, he thought.

He looked up. A being with glowing eyes gave him a moment of pause, as astonishment gave way to drunken, ribald laughter.

Frank had placed two coins over his eyes. They reflected the slanted rays of sunlight beaming in, on dust moat swirls of galactic easygoing, in from outside, where the cons stirred in the yard, whispering, plotting; waiting. The day rose, and the day fell. All was.

"For Charon..." said Frank, and laughed in spite of things.

Printed in Great Britain
by Amazon

35936183R00040